Hearts Higher Than Titles

A Poetry Collection
Written By
Casper Gray

For the Poetizer crowd;
you know who you are.
Before I stumbled my way
into that insatiable app, I had
never known another poet.
I've gotten more enthusiasm
and support from writers there
than I ever expected; I don't
deserve you. But I am
grateful to have you.
Also, for Katie.
I wrote her a poem
one time, wanting to
reach for something
higher than words.
Neither my heart nor
my words will ever
be the same.
Thank you.

Introduction

Love (or perhaps I should say the eternal
pursuit of love) rarely comes across
to me as a fully joyful experience.
Instead it is finding joy in the endless
epiphanies and understandings
that the pain is worth the price
Of having loved. At its worst it is
an impenetrable distance; it is like
The long dark between stars. It is
both the sweet agony of being there and
the torment of not. Then the plagues of
paranoia and insecurity; the pangs of
self doubt and mutual mistrust.
It is everything we wish to promise we
will never be again but for the fact of
being only human. The story these
pages tell are related to the emotions
Of falling in and out of love. A tale of
sunlight, shadow, and of the heart
caught in between. It was agonizing
to choose these because in truth; once
one feels the first stirrings of infatuation
or of love then every action henceforth
becomes intertwined into that. So if

you find my portrait in these pages
seeming every color of dysfunctional
irrationality, then all faults are mine.
I am rather illogical about my heart.

Higher Than Titles

I will hold you sacred between
every word, cradle your image
within every line, raise you
higher than titles.

Paradigm Shift

The first time
he saw her and felt
the world; it was not the same
as the moment before her.
There was no world
before her.

Juliette On The Balcony

Men make hell upon earth in
pursuit of their personal heavens.
At a distance, I have seen mine
in a bright angel tonight; even
if it is only through my begging
eyes, for a steady glimpse
of her moonlit silhouette.

Connecting Skydots

All words were nothing before her.
He saw then, the deep
flecks of diamond light held within–
There were stars at her soul; her gaze,
a night sky, promising constellations–
New shapes to spend his life discovering

First Impressions

It's unfettered wild had never been known.
Indentations like happy scars
on smooth surface;
a whip of thunder at their back,
caught in the first rain that pushed
them indoors; the static over bed sheets,
galvanizing the floor they built storms upon.
Heavy breath entangled within pressed limbs,
becoming hunger against
bodies sinking into easy dark.
Until the bliss and broken
by the first shock of morning; pouring
the night off into the shower drain.
Just being against each other into
hushed whispers; sharing the first coffee,
fumbling for failed words with eyes knowing.
Feeling without words, just first impressions.

August Ravine

They met in the long dried ravine
approaching each other; their muted footsteps
on the blanket of moss beneath them.
Dewy morning still dripped from leaf to leaf,
drops ending soundlessly
into the green carpet underfoot; it was
an ubiquitous second skin of eldritch forest;
a glove of nature, cocooning the murmurs
that made beauty; Sunlight dappled their
interlude upon its dancing.
Neither was lost; they had found each other.
It was an old knowing
entrenched in sapient wonder.
They held each other without
breaking the august quiet.
Fingers digging tight as they
 trembled against one another.

Against The Flame

Myself I never like more
than when I'm with you.
Where the ashes of nights breath
are like a cold hearth stirred into
catching fire heartedly
Within her enfoldedness.
My stumbling speak never selves right,
until my broken quiet is
pried passion within
apart;
we play the language of nothing
everywhere within us.
I am a thoughtful fool; as men think themselves
food for feeling and are wont to be:
Believing the blaze in this night forever.

An Entangle Meant

This changes everything
and fixes nothing; yet I love
how it's her who twines me
into her entangled tomorrows.
I'll admit, I'm a little twisted.
Mostly my heartstrings, she keeps
looped around her fingers like
promise rings, because I
promised her, she can pull
on my dangling need for
her at anytime; puppet
me into foolish feelings.
What I wouldn't do
to damn myself for
her amusement.

Nightlights

Forest chimes as we pass by,
patter strikes a leaves sigh; sky
bends light, trees warping in time.
Dashing grovels the firefly lines.
Fabled stillness lushes alive; the
paved way, our path street-lamped.
Two hands held softly intoxicated
into each others gentleness,
gleamed hopes warmth against
us as we caress through.

I Do Like You

In fact. Everyday
I like you more.
You are the sunlight
I can only ever
imagine from the shade.
To witness your light but
never know your warmth-
I would hold you
even were I incinerated.
Do not take it darkly,
if from time to time I need
to hold my own shadow
in absence of what
I will never have.
But honestly, its
everything you do
not say that burns me.
You mean
everything;
that burns me.

Everything Between

Angel roads, snow once downy soft now
soiled in grime before my trudging footfalls.
My thoughts flake off my brittle brain;
I keep asking God why I have to die.
In truth, I have only just awoken; in life
we die many deaths and in my next phoenix
rise i'll probably feel the same about time.
There is nothing between us, yet everything.
It kills me to live knowing this life is too
short for excuses of what I could not do.
I daydream of running to you, and
have nightmares of never making it.
The daunting contours of distance say
I'll at least be in shape by the time I arrive;
or die, but death is my boggling debt
to life, anyways; it'll fade eventually.
Every horizon holds an ending;
then when I am laid in the morgue
it is the physicians who prepare my
body for burial who will see written
in the lines of my old flesh; the story
of how I loved you when I was alive.

Our Song

We combined our rhythm
together; a moment,
both of us welded into one
from two halves of a single song.
I remember the cool feel
of the airpods we shared
in the first wintry snowfall.
Watching the falling
flakes plunge fatly
as even at a distance
I felt your warmth in the fire.
We held each other in our ears;
the capturing beauty
we pooled tears together to;
It was like you were there,
in my head with me-
And for a composed moment
until the morendo ended;
I fell in love with
Such perfection.

Silken Moon Fireside

Silken moon punctuating
the twilight clearing.
I could fall here
from the threads
of star beams
struggling to dance
through the firelight.
Ribbons of fame
toss shapes;
I know I am lost
forever in the oneness.
This is only for a breath;
a moment between
Lost breaths.

Through Glass

I sleep; with my phone
on my chest; so
it's like I'm keeping you
near my heart.
When it vibrates against me,
I pretend it's your touch.
When it wakes me with a message
from you,
that same heart stills for a second
before the opening in the dark,
when my tired eyes crinkle happily
against the bright screen,
drinking in your light emerging with
the words between us.

                    I am
                Enraptured
              Upon my hearts
          Fulfilment
      At your every
    Single
        Word.
            Hello.

Putty Shapes

One kiss;
i'm melting over her mouth
like a blushing marshmallow.
Her hold;
and I am only silly putty
within the malleable grasp
of her me-shaping hands.
She asks:
"What do I mold you into?"
I whisper back:
"Make me yours."

Love Logged

When she screamed
at me; pushing
against my chest to go; i went.
Later she begged me,
magic in her words.
I held her as she cried, promising
Better
As I was nurturing
the night fire, stoking it,
Knowing I was no better.
Then wondering
into the flames. I saw
our bodies in the burning logs.
Each was a scorching ponder, the question:
Which of us would be the final singe
that splits us as we burn each other alive?

Phantom Edge

Sliding; many bladed
light beams; shearing
dark dreams off of
Nights portraits—
A sun also rises,
it carry's all my
Falling heart; lacerated
above bristling treetops.
They sway hellos as
a sinister breeze
whistles through
whispering leaves.
..I woke; last night I
dreamed you were gone;
my love, lost with you.
A haunt of hunting—
Disquiet from eternities
farsome othered edge.
Hounds of fear follow; space
hollowed empty gasping I wake,
chokes at my periled throat can
not fill enough with the dread

glutting my heart squeezed—
As if racked with choking sobs
or smothered keens unreleased.
If paranoia could spill from my veins
i'd blood let this distance—
What drives me to exist?
When at this dusky dimension
we edge along razored phantoms
wanting to be cleaved in parts
that rivulet their remains
down these final thoughts;
as if I could find your ghost,
then save us both—
Screaming my last
haunting breath to wake
us from this nightmare
in the afterlife.

I'll Rise For You

I am dough for you,
roll me over any surface
and cut from me the
shapes you desire most.
Battered as I am by
Your attentions,
all I want is to rise
to your need,
and be the flavor
that sets you off
and turns your
taste into love
For me.

Fire Flies

I never knew the night until
that first time I watched sparks
peel away from the dusk blanket
to scorch the dark in majesty.
Tiny smears, like dark fabric
rended in weeping flecks of daylight
lamenting it's other half; in perpetual
chase of a full embrace unfulfilled until
it holds her in eclipse once in a blue moon.
I imagined each held a universe
in its glow, popping in and out
of daydreams in the night:
To catch one is to grasp a
forgotten world in your hand.
Hold it to your ear and secrets
whisper eldritch words, to make even
the gods bend a breath in your favor.
One perched on the rim of my jar;
it claimed if I trapped it fast a wish
would be waiting when I needed.
I refused to capture such beauty
within a glass house tragedy,

so it blinked on and off,
fading out of sight.
As it left
it promised me
that I was doomed
to love forever.

Angel Breath

Bright angel;
your silence is a cloud I
would pillow my thoughts upon,
forever; wondering
at your soft essence.
I am all
that shadows
from your radiance.
I would die
Upon your waiting,
to be reborn
on the breath
of your spoken word.
Madness is a man's heart;
to want to need
and to need to want.
You are the cycle;
the wheel that my desire
turns to; lift me
but places I cannot
reach unless you take me
to a bask higher

than words would us,
into a whisper
of new worlds.

Fitting Love

I wish loving someone was
smooth; a puzzle picture to
marvel over the intricacies
of a perfectly assembled image.
I asked for marvel, was shown
to the studio; they told me to
become a broken poet instead
of another tragic avenger.
I asked an AI photo generator,
to paint my broken heart whole;
those images still came out
with a lot of sharp edges.
And if wishes were books we
would all have our own chapter.
I'd still like to cut through all the
bullshit and tie strings binding
every page to the greater story.
I've lived every page I've written,
and sometimes I still struggle to
know where I've placed all
the pieces of my heart.
I need to get them to the

printing press; so when this
goes up in flames too,
I'll still have plenty of
copies to remind me of
who I was.

Head In The Clouds

He'll get there when he does-
Waiting to find her; wanting
towards the other in between
of either chance or fate.
Today he's walking usual;
hands in his pockets,
head in his heart-
Clouds on a clear day
are the story he etches
his dreaming words upon.
Every one is a breath of her,
Shapes of his yearning;
billowing emissaries
blown like cottony thoughts
scouring languid horizons.
Formless silhouettes tickle
at his imaginings; he sees her
in every dusk and dawn.
She is the smile in those hopes;
in the first and last lights
dancing to and fro across steady
distances of pristine possibility.

He hears his own rushing need-
The pounding heart in his ears,
but it is really hers—it for now
it will serve as her voice with
every resonating beat echoing into
the cellular glue that holds him
together; she is ubiquitous in the
ideas that keep him adhered to himself
each like serene gravity binding him to
the inchoate promises strolling leisurely
amongst his whispers into the sky-
Find and shatter me phantom thunder;
we will dance together upon the branches
of lightning that fracture the sky
as we break the world beneath us
with the deafening song of our passion.
Be wary of hushed words; whispers
are taken apart by the slightest breeze.
Who knows where his rising candles
of longing will land; A world
is the heart's true pasture.
But today he's walking usual:
Hands in his pockets,
head in his heart.
Still waiting to find

her at the other end
of chance or fate.
He'll get there
when he does.

Haunting

Through
a haunted darkly
I see, ghostly;
the imaged phantom.
My furthest thoughts scream
into the bane of my inward face,
unable to break free
from this head.
Ideas are the escape—
A mind offers it's light,
but all the stars
in my galaxy
have gone dark.
I chased each one
into every well; of
all -devouring gravity
swallowing every spark
in my soul; eating
my heart also.
It's shadow remains;
everyday—
Beating my brain.

Self-Care

Heavy stubble,
rough as
a sturdy pair of genes
falls from my face
in soft crunches,
like leaving
worried behind.
This is the
elongated moment,
like raindrops in stasis.
I wait for one to fall
from the second
off it's eternal perch.
My heart is in my ears
waiting to rise
with the sound
of her message falling
into my inbox.
It is forever failing
as she no longer replies.
So I decide it's time
to clean myself up;

to quit waiting beside
my phone as my beard grows.
I lose years as it disappears.
weight on my chest lightens
With easier breaths.
Self-nurturing:
the best blessing I
can bestow upon
my needing self.
It will not last the night
but the bath was nice.
My furtive mind
darts my eyes
ever in the direction
my heart will
take downwards
again; again
into the
Inbox.

Sun Swept

My heart is a thirsty straw
slurping sun slushees
from the open eye of day.
It's easier to uncover
my light when the sun
dances off my pale skin,
attaching entangled threads
of early dawn beams
pulling me grounded
over the world I walk upon.
Willowy viridian blades dance away
beneath my first footsteps outside,
bending into smiles;
no longer weeping
with descending dewdrops;
hush humming their content
like windswept whispers-
My mop of hair, restless on my head;
it's dangling strands blown
jovially in the mellow breeze,
as if in sympathy
to my blithe thoughts.

My night sky
no longer sparkles
as it once did;
but there must be
stardust in my lungs-
I can breathe again.

Fallen Fantasy

What she needed; he wanted
to tell her everything; to mean
every hushed breath
as his tongue danced over her,
lapping greedily at her pliable
flesh giving way as they fell further
into whatever space; couch; bed; car;
floor. It could have been any of them.
It was probably all of them; more: Imagine
the breath in her ear, the caress
of soft words as he melted her
further into him "I need you,
there is no one like you, you are
everything. Anything. Always.
You're worth it."

The Vampyres Muse

Pale lips; smug upon the rim
of my brittle wineglass as I imbibe
the final savor of her sanguine gasps;
her lingering essence, misted on my breath.
She dances to the somber haunt of my dead
heart; like mourning cellos at the pavilion.
This masquerade is a swoon, and every
blood brothel is filled; this festival is only
for us beneath the scarlet eye of the moon
wetly glistening, as I stroll atop burgundy waters.
I would trade a single blush of her warmth against
my cold flesh rather than bathe in the rapture of
humanities blood, gathered into an unquenchable
sea from which to slake my eternal thirst upon
forgotten bloodlines; my forsaken heaven awaits.
My tortured Andromeda, held bound by gilded
chains of silver set deeply into the stone beneath.
Crimson jaws await me, the rivulets that
run down her naked skin from lacerations
made by those who would entrap me; in this
riven moment, the debts of invictus damnation
scream for my soul to flee the passing eclipse.

I hold her instead, imagining her hummingbird
heart is beating within me as well; through the
opiate haze of one who has been fed upon,
she whispers against my chest that I should
run ; that her hushed heart will be silenced
regardless; the sapped sunlight already emerges as
the townsfolk sneer across a chasm of our demise;
spectators to our last embrace; our final kiss
before her breathless release as I drink deeply,
my merciful fangs into her cartoid; I am too
drunk upon her to feel as the sun begins crisping
me, my smoldering flesh rising in steam as our
mortal harriers jeer gleefully; our final moments,
I sense when spirits are leaving; my dying agony
is nothing compared to the last light in her
eyes; I capture as it fades and I am in flames
holding onto the memory of her as blackness
swallows the awareness of my charred body
falling into black sand like time overdue.
Then there is nothing, as never could
there be a world before or after her.
There is only her death
and my wind scattered ashes
where once we loved.

Bright Haunt

Angel from my dark fears,
you are both the fantasy and nightmare.
You have gone, but still are here;
in my untethered dreamscapes.
I bite with my spirit into memory,
falling through the conscious onion
of unreality; she is the burning
dreamcatcher above me.
I should remove this dark halo;
hell is already here, it's crown
of pain; I have shoved it's thorns
into my skull
to be the constant kindred to
the hurt I wear to remember you.
It is fleeting, to want to love
and to know need beyond
rationality; your slide into my mind,
already tilted the odds towards insanity.
Now I dine in dark, feasting
upon far light and illusion.

Bright haunt, if even my
eyes were removed, still
I would see only you.

Spider Queen

Dye blue orchids
in vantablack, then
sheath my open grave
with them at dusk.
Fill my lidless casket
to brim with spiders,
that they may
drink of the ink
embalming me,
then be released
from the final prison
of my desiccated corpse.
Pray they spin pale elixir;
silver stranded
storie eyes become
captured in, that
cast the tale of
how my heart
was entangled
in her web even
after my death.

Pale Muse

Give me words; pale muse, I want
to make the gods weep into their wine
who have damned me with love; to seek
that which I cannot have between the lines-
Her phantom echo my heart weeps;
and sings; and dreams.
The restless melancholy of my thoughts;
a constant vigil of mourning lit
between the night of my neurons.
If you must drink, mere gods,
to the strings I dance to as those fates
play my life for you.
Then dredge your ambrosia;
your sweet draught of mortal pain
from the endless well of love
I have poured for her through years,
so I can find the question at the bottom.
To her:
From my heart, I can see see nothing
without also finding you there.
When I found you first love;
what did you ever see in me?

Mistaken Identity

I awoke drowning in heavy waters,
watching my escaping air bubbles pop
to spite me; I thought of them later as
I fried eggs into perfectly round shapes:
The sunny side up; my thoughts captured
within the golden yolk, no wonder
it was so dark in my dreams.
There was a girl last night who mistook
me for Heathcliff; in her high hopes she
Forgot it was grim in Wuthering Heights.
I always find myself sinking into the
pages of what others wish I was,
so when she said she loved me I had
to slam the book shut on myself.
Then I awoke in confusion; forgetting
to inhale as I trembled at blurry shapes
outlined in gray moods asking:
Who am I when I wake?
These jumblesome mindsweeps
of madness taunting as I step
on their awaiting punctuations.

Who am I when I wake?
my words, they do not
seem so much a projection of
me, as I seem
to be an illusion of
all my juggled words
before they drop.

Lecherous Contours

Lust and lecher;
go together.
love is under
though nearly over.
Charming predator;
ensnared within
your own devious flaws.
Sheep and lamb, both
you damn amorously
into their doe eyes.
I am perhaps not as eloquent
although my brain is bright
enough to see contours
within your shadowed facade.
What I know through
my own damned soul:
These dark delights often
bumble light beginnings.
Whether honest rogue
or false brogue,
I require a when
to rest this rumble;

this restless rebuke—
It thrumbles through me
on thunderous bolts
of dreaded doubt.
Men who wear wolfskin
to play powerfully as
lions amongst lambs;
and acceptedly too.
I now near to a leave
beginning to see:
Perhaps this place is
too desperate for me.

Dread Doubts

The poet within me,
following feeling; I'm led
again into dread,
down more dead ends—
What thoughts may destroy,
what muse is my friend?
Damn all these dark dreams,
I lay below the sword of Damocles;
above rest an edge with a promise,
paring my dominant focus upon this—
I once believed, I would see the way
forward, toward any dream I could seem;
astray, only to find me okay; I believed
I was beautiful, then I had to wake—
The bubble popped; the layered waves
I ebb and flow among my dark doubts
and self-assured clarity without promise
of eventuality; I make what every made breaks.
What do my wants matter if I unable to feed
my wants their needs? I would afford this greed
if only to be; the mind that messes with the head,
says I could be played, but the game goes on ahead.

If I stop even a breath; I could catch up to me dead.
I have bled to be me; in both waters high and dry,
my song now is no longer mine; my voice quiet—
Alone as the sole voice in my head keeping me
company; like holding my own hand—
Like sandpaper sounds;
rubbed
against evading desert sands.

A Tango Darkly

Dance with me darkly; we
are as one to each other,
then this beautiful
vainglorious monster—
Like crystal vesper breaths
borne upon winter's chill.
You will find me sheathed
in whispering flickers of fire;
the hatless mad hatter
wearing a suit of cyan flames
for his soul has become both shape
and the sound of sinister contrast.
This raven sky is a peaceful beast,
all the pieces of me pulled
by the last light of dying stars.
I am the puppet of distant gods
fading by their own embrace.
It is the thousand cuts;
the tiny deaths I die in
sight of your outline that
awakens my restless capture
puppeteered; my wandering ghost,

freed in spirit to revel in our
combined unraveling as we
blur like ribbinous shadows
mistaken for sable behemoths
passing overhead.

Broken Botticelli

Every fickle muse in lofty Olympus;
smirking pretty at me behind fluttering fingers
and scrivening fates intoxicated upon my next folly:
Yes, I've been huddled by the ambrosia again.
I could weep into my catalytic cup with
honest passion and I would be applauded
for painting exquisite images off the brush
of every passing thought as I wrenched
your heart from your chest–
Drunken delights, but if I don't
figure out how to breathe you back
to life we'll both be dead by morning.
Pauper prince with a Botticelli pen;
I may not paint but tell me that my words
don't dance images through your thoughts
and I'll raise you two tangos and a line boogie.
This is he; the blushing paleface of dangling
raven hair held back to keep it from itching
his eyes into a watery hell of red rubbing.
And I continue thinking I'm too whatever
to be thought attractive so I keep letting
gazes slide off me when I walk into a room.

I did not know poetry before I knew her;
as one who did not know light before
a sunrise; but whether stars or unrequited
love both are equally out of reach of anything
but a poet's perspective, and thus; the page.
Every fire is for her, yet they all smolder
unattended into extinguishment.
Thus; the next page until the
drink fades and I am stricken
sober enough to mourn
Upon a pen everything
I will never have.

Angel Fall

Ash wings eclipsing
the diluted twilight; fallen
angel; freed from perfection—
Fading pinpricks of Heaven brandish
the world with your dusk even
as I pray to apocryphal gods
that you will descend into my arms.
My thoughts; twisted into the chains
that bind you in your plummet—
My heart; yearning for your abyssal scythe
branded inkly upon nights fragile quilt.
The breath of your plunge; sweeping stars
into stygian ruins in your wake.
You are the scarred heart within
me that I whisper wishes to that
you would cleave into,
so that I may know what it is
to bleed again; to feel once more.
Be the flail bound to my tarnished
soul slendered beyond recognition.
Reach into me with obsidian
tendrils of your darkest dreams,

so that my blood may run black
in rivulets upon the unholy
ground of our rebirth; our
shadows holding each other
until we are damned in death
together when the
sun rises again.

Drunken Rain

Dance the long stumble,
fall drunken rain; tumble
my thoughts in a bottle,
and there goes the pain.
Pitter patter bullets
shooting sky down; the
gravity bound lightning
strikes a frown face now.
Melancholic unease electrics
through me, closing smeary eyes;
my blurry mind is not the same.
Thunder cackles like a
mad hatter who has lost
all his brains.

Doppelgänger

Her scarlet splash; she
sashay's away; a silhouette, darker
then; she whispers on her way: Don't
forget to bring your demons with you.
I pour grim murmurs now into every
tumbler and toast my lackluster shadow:
May the priest be kept at bay for fear
of corrupting my soul again: we pray for
whiskey, but in silent hells of self it only
rains hard water and midnight oil.
Still when falling curses bless into dark
kindling; the pain I scream through the
flames will still be her name. I am not
quite myself, these days I have a shadow
who does not always mimic me, but
reaches out to where my heart
would if it were still free to beat in
more than my doppelgänger inceptions.
I wake again, to crimson kisses, forever sliding
off the edges of my haunted visions; the angel
in my nightmare, the thorn through my hand as
I hand over blood, on the rose of my final words

to that eluding phantasm who was never real.
I could seek therapy; they would
only deal me the same platitudes
the voices in my head do:
my imagination is just
acting up again.

Silent Stars

I used to have words
that mattered more
than others daily prattle.
They blew on the wind
of my thoughts into
her heart, was our sail
expanded for the most
marvelous moment-
Then the pin to our bubble,
I popped it, deflated.
What do I do
if I cannot patch
that empty absence?
Sunlight is silent,
the blithe chimes
I find in my own mind.
My quiet heart can wait
in bleeding stillness
until the falling stars
of my soul are reborn swinging

upon the hinge of her every word.
Open me again; the door
I am through is yours.

Fallen Eve

This is the flickering flame
of my thoughts dancing
around their stalemated shadows.
Hence the tangled symbiotic tango;
these juxtaposed other-entities
keep close, I'm in-between all
of my conflicting discernments—
You may be able to figure out my heart
but you've never seen into my mind.
Emotional madness; the uber-clash
of weeping laughter and hated joys;
the voices, so insecure yet arrogant
feelings come alive thriving off
the echoes of my affirmation—
I hate to love them; I need to hate
their need whispering love as
I hush back a storied sigh—
Listen friend: There was a garden once,
but it's a long way back from Eden.
The uprooted fact of our severed
seed is dual needs; the angel in me

yearns towards the garden; the devil in me
screams it wants to burn it to the ground.
Those hopes; ethereal bands of distant
starlight dims as dark dances close at
the edges of my narrowing vision—
I see demons in both my flame and shadow,
divulging their silky secrets,
flickering enticements into my ear.
Delectable dark, offering its lovers promise:
I'll shudder you with scars,
all the evil you've never felt;
I'll kill everything you love
until I have you to myself.

Iron Man

Falling hard into silent sobs,
years of tears welled back won't fall,
I've chained myself too tightly
to let go without breaking my links.
Now I'm sick with the sadness,
dry heaves choking on past sins-
Still clinging to my obsolete armor.
I once held your heart at my core
for the briefest blink of a lost moment;
I was indestructible as long as I was yours.
What am I now with a shattered shell?
My faith was in the indifference I wore
in self-secure times of ignorant wholeness.
Too close then I forgot we were a universe,
that sooner or later I would have to find the
strength to weather the long dark between stars.
Step out of my mind; back here on Earth
you are the song in every warble off
of a falling raindrop; I am drenched
where once liquid bullets of feeling
would bounce off in blissful laughter.
I'd ask a passerby to share their umbrella,
but my heart still dances after

your every striking rhythm-
A part of us has run into the ground
but I am still falling among memory.
Every note is a blistering melody;
I am sheened in your music; listening
over and over to the mournful symphony's.
Others might run to get out of the rain
but I would rather blast the pain,
drowning at max volume until;
My naked soul is bare-
Then stand again numb,
and keep moving on.

Insurmountable

You are the infinite wall in all my vision,
my entire being aches trying to scale
the heights of the tower you hide within.
You see, perspective is everything.
My fortress would crumble to let you in
though it seems superfluous to say this,
when my gate is always open for you.
Yours is slammed shut
as you silently scream for others
to try harder to earn their way towards you.
Every breath of any word of mine is yours;
how can you hear it when you won't let me near?
Perhaps I should slit my wrists scaling
your sharp walls, throw myself
plummeting over the other side,
pull my broken self up and write
your name in my blood
before my dying heart spills
your image onto my last breath
taking the shape of your face.
Maybe that would be
enough for you.

Blithe Heart

My eyes weeping waters
from this lonely affliction,
sealed inside this bubble afloat
I am stolen upon;
through a clashing sky,
of desires both distant and close.
Finding her, I was lifted;
we danced through the sky
in sweeping maneuvers
and aerial oddities.
We crashed into one another,
our translucent feelings
we held on to with hope,
popped like illusions
as the ground caught our fall;
the released waters
of past tears plummeting
back upon us in this present.
We crawled
in opposite directions
away from the circumfluence;
the watery grave we made

for ourselves,
to save ourselves
from drowning within
our own emotional tides.
I still want to find you–
even as I wander away
I listen for your echo
to call me back.
My dream of you
is a compass.
Memory is the dreamcatcher
confusing the direction.
The pointed signpost
in my soul says:
Go where your heart is
and there will you be also.
When I am gone
no one will know
who I really was,
they will only remember
What I did for love.

Something I'm Proud Of

High spider strands glistening;
like silky diamond ropes glinting
as an easy breeze sways them–
My hopes; my hair; the treetops,
all bending to the wind with
the field of dancing grass blades
before me; they were there, hushing
whispers across expanses; my fingers
running through the unshucked wheat.
And I am ambling again,
my heart in freefall; free
at last yet still sinking in
bittersweet feeling.
My mind is borne
upon a balmy wind.
I can't be proud of me
in my aftermaths.
My faith in people
tilts like golden wheat
stalks before my gentle touch.
So I pick a fat grass blade and whistle
thanks through it before letting

it tumble back down to earth.
It's a nice day. I move forward.
I'm proud of that.

Unspoken Links

We kindred souls in silence
connected ; remember me in
morning as I rise at a distance and
know I would love to be your sun.
You have been all the radiance
dilating these pupils so I could
see more clearly into my soul.
Then I'll still be thinking of you
when the pine needles here drop off
tired trees and they crunch thoughtfully
beneath my footsteps under the first snowfall.
Reminding me of all the falling thoughts
of you that I could never reach.
And it is every I love you
i've never said that
makes it hardest
to let go.

A Memory Of Lunelight

His breath against night like witchcraft;
he keeps it, slung across his shoulders.
Threads of silken moonlight burn coldly
over calm waters in quivering pale embers.
Resting himself on a rocky protrusion; he
unholsters his weapon of choice, settling.
The hole in his guitar is an eye where his
heart should be looking out into magic.
So he is only alive when his heart's strings
are plucked to thrum in self-entunement.
Maybe a picture is worth a thousand
words, but so is silence worth a
thousand considerations before
the first strum. Then the broken quiet
and she becomes diaphanous strands
dancing into coalescing star strikes
refracting themself through the brittle
glass of his reflection rippling on water.
She kicks up moon dust to glisten
upon beams of bending starlight playing
the quavering night through every chord.
Even the restless waters holding her ghost

still to listen as shadows incline forth to
also hear the memories casting them.
But no one knows it but him; as
only I knew you were there; dancing
upon a lily pool of moonlight
as I played us into an ephemeral
embrace a final time, as only—
I know now that
You're gone.

About The Author

Casper Gray lives in the Midwest.
He has never been to Hogwarts
but tries to infuse magic into all of his words.
Although being a rock star is
actually his dream job, the page keeps calling
and writing seems to be his chosen calling.
He plays guitar and devours sci-fi novels in his spare time.
He writes only non-fiction.
All his stories are true.
Even if they only take place in your head or heart.

Made in the USA
Coppell, TX
20 June 2023

18301202R00049